121 Express

121 Express

Monique Polak

Currents

ORCA BOOK PUBLISHERS

Library and Archives Canada Cataloguing in Publication

Polak, Monique
121 express / Monique Polak.
(Orca currents)

ISBN 978-1-55143-978-5 (bound)--ISBN 978-1-55143-976-1 (pbk.)

I. Title. II. Title: One hundred twenty-one express. III. Series.
PS8631.O43O54 2008   JC813'.6   C2007-906844-8

First published in the United States, 2008
Library of Congress Control Number: 2007940721

Summary: Lucas enjoys his status as a troublemaker on the school bus until the
consequences become serious.

FSC MIX
Paper from
responsible sources
FSC® C016245

*Orca Book Publishers is dedicated to preserving the environment and has
printed this book on paper certified by the Forest Stewardship Council®.*

Orca Book Publishers gratefully acknowledges the support for its
publishing programs provided by the following agencies: the Government
of Canada through the Canada Book Fund and the Canada Council for the Arts,
and the Province of British Columbia through the BC Arts Council
and the Book Publishing Tax Credit.

Cover photography by Corbis Images

ORCA BOOK PUBLISHERS
PO Box 5626, Stn. B
Victoria, BC Canada
V8R 6S4

ORCA BOOK PUBLISHERS
PO Box 468
Custer, WA USA
98240-0468

www.orcabook.com
Printed and bound in Canada.

15 14 13 12 • 6 5 4 3

For Nicholas Lighter, sunshine itself

Montreal Transit Corporation
800 de la Gauchetière
Montreal, Quebec

August 4, 2006

Lorne Crest Academy
4243 Decelles Ave.,
Ville St. Laurent, Quebec
Att.: John Mallard, Principal

Dear Mr. Mallard,

As you are well aware Lorne Crest students who ride the 121 Express bus have a history of misbehavior. Our drivers have had to contend with swearing, shouting, fights and vandalism. Your students, ordinary youngsters when they are not on the bus, turn into—if I may permit myself to use the term—monsters when they ride the 121 Express.

In cooperation with the local school boards, the Montreal Transit Corporation provides express bus service at over twenty-five schools.

Nowhere else have we experienced the problems our drivers report having with your monst…I should say, students.

I write to you with the hope that there will be no such further problems in the coming school year. I implore you to distribute this letter to all Lorne Crest Academy students as well as their parents.

We at the Montreal Transit Corporation pride ourselves on the fine service we provide Montrealers. We believe riding our buses is a privilege. Please make your students understand that if their behavior this year is not acceptable, we will have no choice but to put an end to service on the 121 Express bus.

May I take this opportunity to wish you a successful academic year.

Sincerely,

Jacques Lebrun,
President,
Montreal Transit Corporation

Chapter One

I tried not to act nervous. I took a deep breath, straightened my back and stepped onto the 121 Express. Everyone says it's hell on wheels. The principal even sent around this letter from the Transit Corporation warning that if kids on the bus don't behave, they'll pull the service. Then we'll all have to walk home, which would be really bad for me since our new house is all the way in Ahuntsic. It would take me over an hour to walk home.

The first thing I noticed when I got on the bus was the stench of sweat—and rotten eggs. I ducked when a sandwich came flying like a Frisbee and landed on the floor near my feet. When the kid behind me stepped on the sandwich, mashed-up egg salad splattered in every direction.

I knew I didn't have much time to pick a seat. The main thing when you're a new kid is not to draw attention to yourself.

It only took me a few seconds to figure out how the seating worked. The cool guys—the soccer jocks and the troublemakers—sat at the back. There were a few girls there too. One had changed out of her school kilt into skintight jeans.

The nerds sat up front. They were easy to spot, because they stared at the floor, hoping nobody would pick on them. There was also a higher percentage of kids with glasses in the nerd section. One had a textbook propped open on his lap, but I knew he was just pretending to read. Who could read with all that noise—and sandwiches flying through the air?

"You big loser!" some guy at the back hollered out the window. "What? You didn't hear me? I said you're a big loser!"

The girl in the jeans slapped the guy sitting next to her. "Don't you touch me!" she said, but then she started laughing.

I shook my backpack off my shoulders and grabbed a spot near the middle of the bus, next to a redheaded girl. For now, I figured, the middle of the bus was about where I belonged.

But I was planning to change that. I hadn't exactly been popular at my old school.

This was my new beginning—my second chance. I was going to get in with the cool guys—no matter what. It was just a matter of making my personal life my top priority.

The redheaded girl's MP3 player had a peace sticker on it. She moved closer to the window when I sat down.

I wasn't going to stare at the floor like one of the nerds. So I stuffed my backpack under my seat and looked around—as discreetly as possible. One of the nerds, Sandeep Singh— I knew his name because he was in my English class—took a break from staring at the floor to adjust his black turban. When he saw me looking at him, he nodded.

I looked away. The last thing a new guy needs is a nerdy friend.

I turned around when I heard this loud peal of laughter coming from the back of the bus. It was Miss Tight Jeans. "How many times do I have to tell you not to touch me, Georgie?"

"How many times do I have to tell you not to touch me?" the troublemakers called out, in high-pitched imitations of her voice.

"I don't sound like that!" she shrieked.

"Oh, yes you do, Kelly! That's exactly what you sound like. 'How many times do I have to tell you not to touch me?'" Georgie said. He had dark eyes and dark hair. I spotted a small Greek flag on the arm of his jean jacket.

Up front, more kids shuffled onto the bus. Soon there'd be only standing room.

Two nerdy girls elbowed each other when this guy I recognized from math got on. "Look, it's Jake," I heard one of

7

the girls whisper. "Doesn't he look just like Zac Efron?"

"I forgot my pass," Jake muttered to the driver.

The driver ran his fingers through his thin silver hair. "I can't let you on. Rules are rules." He sounded like he'd had a rough day.

"Not even this once?"

When the driver shook his head, Jake shrugged. But before he got off the bus, he turned back to the driver. "What a jerk!" he called out.

The driver didn't say anything, but even from where I was sitting, I noticed how his cheek twitched.

Someone slid open a window at the back of the bus. "Hey, Jake!" a voice called, and then whoever it was threw Jake their bus pass.

Three seconds later, Jake was back. "I found it," he said, grinning as he flashed the pass at the driver.

"Let me have a look at that picture," the driver said.

But Jake was already lost in the crowd. I couldn't see him, but I could hear him high-fiving the guy who'd lent him his bus pass. "You're my man, Pierre," Jake said.

Maybe it was the heat from so many bodies, but the egg smell was getting worse. Some kids at the back were hurling pieces of scrunched-up paper. One hit the girl next to me. The name Valerie was engraved on her bracelet. "Oww!!" she said, extra loud because she was talking over her MP3 player.

"Cut it out!" the driver shouted. He might have said it again, but I couldn't tell for sure over all the noise.

In a weird way, I was having fun. When some of the kids around me started laughing, I laughed too. I reached for the ball of paper that had landed on the floor and threw it as hard as I could toward the back of the bus.

"Hey, new guy!" a voice called. "You pitch like a girl!"

I bristled. It was my own fault; I'd called attention to myself.

I knew whatever I did next was important. This was what my mom would call a defining moment. She says life is all about defining moments, only most people miss them. They're too busy doing other stuff.

I knew if I acted embarrassed or afraid, the kids at the back would peg me as a loser. If I could come up with a smart comeback, I'd be saved. But there was too much pressure. I couldn't think of anything smart to say.

I felt Sandeep Singh's eyes on me, waiting to see what I'd do next.

So I did the only thing I could to save myself.

I turned to Sandeep. "What are you looking at, raghead?" I asked in a loud voice. Sandeep squirmed, but the kids at the back cracked up. At least the pressure was off me.

As the bus turned onto Côte-Vertu Boulevard, I remembered our science teacher said we'd be studying Charles Darwin's theory of natural selection this year. She told us how Darwin believed only the fittest creatures survive.

Darwin was onto something. A kid's got to be fit to survive the 121 Express.

Chapter Two

I heard the vice principal's high heels clicking down the hallway before I saw her. "Good luck on curbside duty today, Andrew," she told Mr. Adams when she passed him. Then she lowered her voice and added, "The monsters are always at their worst on the Friday before a long weekend."

Mr. Adams groaned. "Thanks for the heads up." But the vice principal didn't hear him. Her heels were already clicking out the side door. I guess she was as happy to leave school as the rest of us.

Monday was a day off—which meant we had three free days in a row. We had a bit of homework, but nothing that couldn't get done on Monday night. And though it was only week three of school, I'd made some friends. Guys like Jake and Pierre from the back of the bus.

I'd had to cause a bit of trouble to get in with them, but it was worth it. The first thing I did was stick a wad of pink chewing gum on the bus driver's seat. When he got up to stretch his legs, it looked like he had a long pink tail. The guys thought that was pretty funny.

Then last week, I brought along a water pistol I'd filled with 7-Up and squirted a couple of the nerdy girls. You should have heard them shriek. This one Asian girl, Jewel Chu, was jumping up and down she was so angry. "I'm going to send you my dry cleaning bill!" she said. But I just laughed.

And yesterday, I insulted an old lady's car when she pulled up next to the bus. "Your clunker's got more rust than metal on it!" I yelled out the window. When the old lady turned her head, I realized it was Mrs. Gibbs, my old kindergarten teacher. I ducked so she wouldn't notice me.

Today, when the bell rang at three, the mood at the bus lineup was extra crazy. Kelly and her friends were dancing, and Pierre punched one of the nerds in the stomach. The kid was lying on the ground moaning, but he stopped when Mr. Adams walked by.

"Everything okay?" Mr. Adams asked as he helped the kid up from the sidewalk. "You look a little winded."

"Yup, everything's fine."

When the bus doors opened, we stampeded past Mr. Adams, who was standing at the curb, shaking his head. This time Pierre couldn't find his bus pass, so the two of us pushed our way in through the back doors.

I saw the bus driver eyeing us in his rearview mirror. It was a cool September day, but his forehead was sweaty. "Hey, hey," he called out, but nobody paid any attention.

When Jake raised his lighter in the air, I took mine out too. We all had lighters, even if we didn't smoke. We liked snapping them. The driver couldn't take the sound—and he was probably afraid we were going to set fire to his precious bus.

"Look!" someone called out from the front of the bus. "The driver's cheek is twitching double-time!"

Soon all of us at the back were snapping our lighters. Then Kelly and her friends started pulling on the yellow cord that makes the bell ring. Between the snapping and the ringing, it was like a bad concert. Everyone was laughing. Even old Sandeep Singh.

Everyone, that is, except the bus driver. When he swerved around this Subaru wagon, so close he nearly took off the sideview mirror, I thought he was losing it.

"Hey, man, I think it's time for some driving lessons!" Jake called out.

"Yeah, what are you trying to do— kill us?" Kelly shrieked.

The driver's back was straight as a stick. I could tell he was trying to focus on the road. Then, with no warning at all, he pulled over to the side of Côte-Vertu Boulevard and turned on the emergency lights. Their steady tick-tick echoed like a clock inside the bus.

Other drivers honked for us to get out of their way. But instead the driver put the engine into neutral and rose from his seat.

Except for the ticking, the bus was dead quiet.

The driver ran his fingers through his gray hair. "You kids are in a big hurry to start your weekend, right?"

"We sure are," Jake called out. "So you driving us to the metro, or what?"

The driver just stood there, staring at us. His belly hung over his pants like a spare tire, and he was breathing hard. "I'm not driving you nowhere unless you cut out your nonsense. No lighters, no bells. No nothing. Got that?" He practically spit out the words.

The nerds all nodded. But the driver knew their word wasn't good enough. "What about you guys at the back?"

Jake stood up and walked to the center of the bus so he was facing the driver. Everyone's eyes were on Jake. A couple of girls at the front of the bus twittered.

"Sure thing," Jake said.

The driver waddled back to his seat. When Jake turned around, he gave us a wink. We all knew that meant Trouble. With a capital T.

Chapter Three

If you're looking for a soccer ball, chances are Pierre's got one. Today the ball was between his knees. Pierre was using it to exercise his quads.

All Jake had to do was point. Pierre released the ball. Then he tossed it up in the air and used the top of his head to butt it over to Jake.

Jake yelped as he head-butted the ball halfway down the bus.

"Keep it going!" voices shouted.

"You'd better watch it!" Jewel Chu said.

Things could've gone worse. The ball could have hit the driver, and he could have lost control of the bus.

Instead the ball hit Jewel Chu, breaking one of her pink finger-nails—the ones she spent most of English class filing. Still it was just a nail, though from the sounds of it, you'd have thought we'd stolen one of her young.

Jewel leapt up from her seat. When she turned around, I noticed how the vein that ran across the middle of her forehead was throbbing. "I can't believe you broke my nail! You guys are total imbeciles!"

Sandeep Singh watched the action from the corner of his eye.

I grinned. For me, being called a total imbecile was a compliment.

We expected the bus driver to pull over and give us another lecture, only he didn't. Instead he picked up speed. For a few minutes, the 121 Express was flying! We held onto the bottoms of our seats—or the closest pole. The driver's window was open, and his gray hair flapped in the breeze. I figured he was in a hurry to reach the Côte-Vertu metro station, where most of the kids who take the 121 Express get out.

Jake was standing on one of the seats at the back. His sneakers had already left gray scuff marks on the vinyl. "Hey, Lucas," he called, "I need some help."

I went over to see what he wanted. When the bus squealed to a stop at a red light, we nearly fell over. Luckily, Jake grabbed onto one of the gray rubber handgrips—and I hung on to Jake.

The two of us must have looked like a couple of monkeys swinging from a banana tree.

When the bus jerked forward, we got back to work. I was helping Jake pop open the emergency ceiling window. The trick was to undo the levers on either end.

"What kind of useless emergency window is this?" Jake shouted when the window wouldn't budge. "Lemme out of here! I can't breathe!! This is an emergency!" Then he started making choking noises and pounding his chest, which cracked everyone up.

"Hey, Kelly," I shouted, "I think Jake needs some mouth-to-mouth resuscitation!"

That made everyone laugh even harder.

"Let me put on my lip-gloss first!" Kelly shouted.

When the window finally popped open, it made a noise like a burp. "Yes!" Jake hollered. He pushed the window open as wide as it could go.

A burst of cool air came jetting through the bus. We must have passed some big trees because a few bright red maple leaves came flying down too.

We stuck our heads through the opening and screamed like madmen. "We're gonna die!" we yelled. "We're gonna die!"

The bus driver picked up even more speed. Wasn't he worried about the cops pulling him over?

Someone was rushing down the aisle. I slid down from the window to see what was going on. Jewel Chu was clutching the soccer ball against her chest.

"You show him!" one of her friends called out.

"I wanted to return this to you." Jewel threw the ball at Jake's stomach. Hard.

Jake fell down from the window, moaning when he hit the floor.

The soccer ball rolled to the floor too. "At least you didn't break a nail," Jewel muttered.

Pierre wanted his ball back.

"I'll give it back to you all right!" Then Jewel bent down and unfastened the safety pin from her kilt.

Jewel raised the pin in the air like a spear; then she stabbed Pierre's soccer ball. Pierre's mouth fell open and his silver braces gleamed in the afternoon sun.

"Here you go," Jewel said in this syrupy-sweet voice. She handed Pierre what was left of his soccer ball.

"Why'd you have to go and do that?" Pierre asked.

"Why'd you have to go and break my nail?"

"I didn't break your nail."

Someone laughed. It was a laugh we didn't recognize at first. There was something haunted about the sound of it. It took us a few seconds to realize it was the driver. He'd been watching the action in the rearview mirror.

The brakes squealed when the driver pulled up in front of the metro. The doors opened and almost everyone piled out, except for me and a few other kids who lived farther along Côte-Vertu Boulevard.

"That was the worst ride we ever had," I heard Jewel Chu say as she stood up to leave.

Jake, who was standing behind her, patted the top of Jewel's head. "Funny, I thought it was pretty cool."

Jewel stopped when she reached the driver. "Thank you, sir," she said, flashing him a bright smile. "Have a wonderful weekend."

The bus driver didn't say a thing. He just stared into space like a zombie.

Chapter Four

Jake waved at me before he disappeared into the metro station with Pierre. "See ya tomorrow," he said, mouthing the words.

Tomorrow, Pierre and I were both invited over to Jake's to play some b-ball and have pizza. Life was definitely looking up. In a way, I owed it all to the

121 Express. It was where I'd first made friends with Jake and Pierre.

So what if my marks weren't what they'd been at Lasalle Regional? The main thing was I had friends. Cool friends.

I leaned back into my seat. Kelly Legault had carved her initials into the window.

It was much quieter now that the bus was nearly empty. For the first time since I got on, I could hear noises coming from outside: birds chirping, cars honking, and somewhere in the distance, the whine of an ambulance siren.

The emergency window was hanging open. I could have shut it, but I didn't. Something about seeing it like that made me feel good. It reminded me of the fun Jake and I had had prying it open and then screaming our heads off. I could still hear the laughing when I'd made that joke about Kelly needing to give Jake mouth-to-mouth resuscitation. Sometimes, I thought, as I gazed out the window, I could be pretty funny.

When the driver drove through a yellow light, I moved closer to the front. I didn't want to miss my stop.

I could have taken one of the empty seats up front but I didn't. I'd worked too hard to earn my place at the back, and I felt like it would be bad luck to sit with the nerds. So I just stood there, clutching a pole. If the driver took a sharp turn now, I wouldn't lose my balance.

Valerie and Sandeep were still riding the bus too. I knew Valerie got off at the stop before mine. From where I was standing, I could see the way her red hair frizzed up at the ends. It was a nice color of red. For once she wasn't listening to her MP3 player. She was writing in a fat spiral notebook.

She must have felt me watching because she closed the notebook and stuffed it inside her backpack.

"What are you doing—writing a book?" I asked.

I knew she'd heard me, but she just turned toward the window and sighed. I figured she wanted to steer clear of troublemakers—and I liked that she thought I was one of them. Even if it meant she was ignoring me.

Sandeep was sitting on one of the long seats behind the driver, watching us. "Hey, Valerie," he said.

It kind of bothered me when Valerie turned around for Sandeep. "What's up?" she asked him.

"Not much. I'm excited about that project Mr. Adams wants us to do—the one about modern-day heroes. Did you pick your hero yet?"

Jeez, I thought, Sandeep really needed lessons in how to be cool.

Imagine telling a girl you're excited about an English project.

But Valerie actually seemed interested. "I'm thinking about doing Mahatma Gandhi," she said. "He believed in nonviolence." She raised her voice when she said that, which made me think she was trying to tell me something.

"I'm all for nonviolence," I said. I hadn't meant to say anything.

Valerie sighed again. "Messing with the emergency window is violence—kind of, anyway."

"No, it's not," I said quickly. "We didn't hurt anyone."

"What about him?" Sandeep raised his dark eyebrows toward the bus driver.

"I can't help it if he can't drive." I said it loud enough for the driver to hear me. His cheek twitched.

When Valerie started discussing Mahatma Gandhi again—how a lot of

31

people think he was related to Indira Gandhi, who was prime minister of India, only they weren't related at all— I knew it meant my part in the conversation was over.

I was sorry I'd said anything at all. I was better off ignoring those two—the way they were ignoring me.

The driver slowed down before Valerie's stop. Valerie said good-bye to Sandeep, but she ignored me altogether. I tapped on the pole and pretended not to notice.

I had to crane my neck to watch Valerie walk down Côte-Vertu Boulevard, her head held high. She wasn't very friendly. But I still liked the color of her hair.

Sandeep took a book from his backpack. I figured it was a physics or math textbook, but it wasn't. It was a new thriller by Michael Connelly, and from the looks of it, Sandeep was into it.

I liked Michael Connelly too. He was the kind of writer who made you feel you were there with him—inside his story.

About a block before my stop, I reached up to tug on the bell cord. I had a feeling the driver wouldn't slow down the way he had for Valerie. Sandeep usually got off at my stop too, but for now, he was still sitting, lost in his book.

I went to the very front of the bus and waited behind the tinted glass that separated the driver from his passengers. That little space, I thought, that didn't measure more than a few square feet, was the guy's office.

The driver's hands had brown spots and his bony fingers shook when he gripped the wheel.

Sandeep was busy reading. "Hey," I called out, "it's our stop!"

Sandeep stood up, but he didn't shut his book.

The driver pulled up to our stop. I could have thanked him, but I didn't. What stopped me was the idea of what the guys would say if they knew.

As I got off, I felt Sandeep's weight on the step behind me. When I stopped to toss my empty water bottle into the garbage can by the bus stop, I half expected Sandeep to stop too. He wasn't cool, but I didn't see any harm in walking a couple of blocks with the guy.

Only Sandeep didn't stop. He just kept reading his book, which he had balanced in one hand.

What a loser, I thought, as he walked right past me.

Chapter Five

Mr. Adams was on curb patrol. That meant we could pretty much do whatever we wanted as long as no one got thrown into the street and run over by a car. Mr. Adams was one of the youngest teachers at Lorne Crest. I guess he still remembered what being a kid felt like.

Mr. Adams gave me a high five when he saw me waiting with Jake and Pierre. "Hey, Lucas," he said, "I was talking to my cousin, Jeanette, over the weekend. She teaches at Lasalle Regional."

Uh-oh. Jeanette Adams had been my grade six English teacher. Now that I thought about it, she and Mr. Adams looked alike. They were both short, with dark skin and dark almond-shaped eyes.

"She told me your nickname, and to be honest, Lucas, it took me by surprise."

My body stiffened. Uh-oh, I thought. Now the guys are going to know the truth: Before I came to Lorne Crest, I was as nerdy as Sandeep Singh. I tried staring at Mr. Adams, hoping that would make him stop, but he didn't get the message. My face felt hot.

Jake rocked on the balls of his feet. "So what was Lucas's nickname?"

I remembered the fun I'd had at Jake's on Saturday and wondered if I'd ever get invited over there again.

Mr. Adams slapped me on the back. "Brainiac," he said.

I gulped. Maybe I could talk my way out of this. "I—uh—don't think so. Your cousin must've mixed me up with someone else."

"I don't think so either," Pierre piped in. "Not with the mark he just got on our science quiz."

Mr. Adams's eyes narrowed. "I get it," he said, nodding. "Jeanette must have you mixed up with someone else. Someone with a brain."

That made the other guys laugh. "Luke's got a brain," Jake said, elbowing me, "only he hardly ever uses it."

Pierre was pulling out an ad from one of the Plexiglas holders over the windows.

The ad had a blue and white peace sign on it.

Georgie laughed as he read the wording: "*Paix sur l'autobus. Paix sur la terre.*" That was French for "Peace on the bus. Peace on Earth."

"What a joke!" Georgie said.

Valerie shot Georgie a dirty look. Judging by the sticker on her MP3 player, she was pretty serious about the subject of peace.

Once Pierre fished the whole ad out, he tore it into ribbons and passed the ribbons around. The rest of us scrunched the paper into balls and hurled them toward the front of the bus. Some of the kids at the front tried ignoring us; others threw the paper balls back at us. It was almost as good as a snowball fight.

Jewel Chu's eyes widened, and when she covered her mouth with her hand, I started to wonder what was freaking her out. As I turned around, I heard a chorus of "oohs" and then Jewel saying, "That's so gross! How could she?"

Kelly Legault, who was sitting two rows behind me, had climbed onto Georgie Papadopoulos's lap and was checking out his tonsils. At least that's what it looked like.

That Kelly Legault was hot all right. I couldn't help wondering what kissing a girl that way would feel like. Pretty good, I guessed.

"Free show!" Jake called out.

Then everyone at the back started clapping. Jewel Chu looked like she was about to throw up.

When the bus stopped at a red light, Jake nudged me. "Hey, Brainiac," he said, handing me a tub of yogurt. "I dare you to dump this on that car's windshield. Jake used his chin to point at a shiny black Nissan with tinted windows. It looked like it had come straight from the car wash.

One of the things about hanging out with the cool guys is that sometimes you have to make split-second decisions. This, I realized, was one of those times. If I said no, Jake would think I was a wimp. And who knew what kind of trouble I could get into if I said yes?

If only the light would turn green.

But it stayed red.

Pierre's pale blue eyes were shining. "Go for it, man!" he said.

I took a deep breath and grabbed the plastic tub from Jake. "Just don't call me Brainiac!"

Jake grinned. Then he leaned over and opened the window a little wider.

Now other kids were watching me too. I guess they were bored of gawking at Kelly and Georgie.

"Come on!" Pierre called out.

There were other voices too, egging me on. "Yeah, Lucas, do it!"

The last thing I noticed as I threw the tub of yogurt out the window was that it was field berry. It seemed like a weird thing to notice.

I'd aimed for the middle of the Nissan's windshield. I couldn't help feeling proud when I saw the yogurt tub explode as it made contact with the glass. A second later, the entire windshield was splattered with pink goop.

Jake clapped my back.

"Look what he did!" someone at the front of the bus called out.

The kids at the back were all laughing. They laughed even harder when the driver of the Nissan turned on his windshield wipers. Now there were goopy pink arcs on the windshield. "He's only making it worse!" Pierre yelled.

Even though throwing the yogurt was probably the worst thing I'd ever done, it felt good. Liberating, I guess you could say.

But this other part of me was watching the traffic light. It was still red. Was it broken or what?

What happened next seemed to take place in slow motion—the way bad things usually do. The door to the Nissan popped open. A man with a flushed face, wearing a shirt and tie, got out.

I felt a pit at the bottom of my stomach.

The light was still red.

The man made a fist.

The light turned green. Gun it, I thought, hoping somehow the driver would hear my wish. But he didn't gun it.

He yanked on the hand brake. The man with the tie marched over to the front of the bus. He raised his palm in the air like he was directing traffic.

"Hey, this is great!" Jake shouted. "Better than the movies!"

I wasn't so sure.

Chapter Six

The bus driver sighed as he opened the front door. The rest of us watched in silence as the man climbed onto the bus, taking two steps at a time. He was breathing hard. So was I.

Jake had slid the window shut. Was it my imagination or were there pinkish specks on my seat? Could it be field berry yogurt?

I thought about switching seats, but of course, it was too late for that. If I stood up, I'd look suspicious. So I leaned as far back into my seat as I could.

The man headed straight for the driver. "Who the hell threw that yogurt at my car?" His face was almost as red and shiny as the traffic light that hadn't changed in time.

The driver shrugged. "I wish I knew. They're all monsters—especially the ones at the back."

Once he realized the driver couldn't help him, the man turned to the rest of us. His voice boomed as if it was coming through a loudspeaker: "Do you understand how dangerous this could have been? I couldn't see out my window! I could have caused an accident! People could have gotten hurt!" When he raised his arm in the air, I noticed a ring of sweat under his armpit.

I tried not to squirm, even when Kelly uncrossed her long legs and winked at me.

"I demand to know who did it! Who threw that yogurt?" The man looked toward the back of the bus, eyeing every single one of us. Somehow I managed to meet his gaze.

I wondered who would turn me in. Sandeep? It would be a way for him to get even for me calling him raghead on the first day. Jewel? She was just the type to rat out another kid. Valerie? She thought I was a personal enemy of Mahatma Gandhi. Or maybe one of my friends from the back of the bus? Someone who'd tell on me just for the fun of it.

But no one said a word.

The man reached into his pocket for his cell phone. "If you don't tell me who's responsible, I'm going to call the police!" he said, snapping the phone open.

Uh-oh, I thought. Now I'm cooked. I imagined the police hauling me off the bus. Then I imagined my parents' faces when they'd get the news. Their son—their only child, the one who, up to this year, had been a model student—arrested for public mischief.

I tried not to move. But now, other kids were squirming. I looked over at the front of the bus. Jewel was chewing her lip. Sandeep was buried in a textbook.

No one was going to turn me in.

The driver got up from his seat and put his hand on the man's shoulder. "You're not going to get anything out of these kids. The monsters have a code of silence. And phoning the police won't get you anywhere, either."

The man made another fist and shook it in the air. "You might have gotten away with it this time, whoever you are.

But take it from me—life's gonna catch up with you. And it'll make you pay."

"Hey, that's pretty funny—life's gonna make you pay!" Jake jabbed me in the ribs.

Pierre's shaggy head poked up from the seat behind us. "That guy's a real nut," he said. "I mean it's not like anything happened. Maybe he just doesn't like yogurt!"

"Maybe he's got a milk allergy!" Kelly added.

The light was red again, but when it turned green, the bus driver didn't move.

"Hey, what's going on?" Jake called out.

The driver was hunched over the wheel. But then he stood up and turned to face us. "Look," he said in a quiet voice, "I've had it with you monsters.

That guy was right—someone could have been hurt just now. So I've made a decision: I'm not driving you anywhere today. You're on your own. Get the hell off my bus!"

Jewel gasped. I couldn't tell if it was because the driver was kicking us off the bus or because he'd used the word *hell*.

There was grumbling everywhere—up front, in the middle and at the back where I was sitting. "I'm going to be late for my piano lesson," I heard Sandeep say.

We all waited a few minutes before getting off the bus—in case the driver changed his mind the way our parents sometimes did when they got angry. But he didn't. He just sat there, tapping his foot on the floor, and not looking at any of us when we finally filed out of the bus.

We walked to the metro station in a pack. It took twenty minutes, even though we were hoofing it.

Valerie was up ahead. When we stopped for a red light, I saw her balance on one leg to kick off a shoe. Then she leaned down to examine her heel. She must have had a blister. When she caught me looking at her, she glared.

Jake had thrown his arm over my shoulder. "Hey, that was cool, man!" he said. "I'll never forget how red that guy's face was when he got on the bus."

"Or the way the yogurt smeared under the wipers," Pierre added, laughing.

I couldn't see Sandeep. He must have started running to get to his piano lesson.

I decided not to feel guilty. I might have tossed the yogurt at the guy's car, but in a way, I told myself, we'd all done it. Every single one of us.

Chapter Seven

The whole bus reeked of burnt plastic. "Ick," Jewel Chu called out, wrinkling her nose. Valerie slid open a window to let in some fresh air.

Georgie and Pierre had used their lighters to melt the plastic bell cord. Part of the plastic had melted right off. In a couple of spots, you could see right down to the wire.

The bus driver coughed so hard I thought he might let go of the wheel.

Burning the cord was Georgie's idea. I think he came up with it because he and Kelly were in a fight—something about him forgetting to phone her—and he wanted to take his mind off of her.

In the meantime, Kelly was cozying up to Jake.

"Hey," we heard her ask him, "did you get a haircut?"

"Uh-huh. Actually, I got them all cut."

That cracked Kelly up. "You look really good," she told Jake.

From the way Jake laughed, you could tell he was embarrassed.

"My back's killing me from gymnastics. D'you think you could rub it for me?"

Jake shot a look at Georgie, but Georgie was busy with the bell cord, burning another spot. There wasn't any orange flame, but you could see more of the plastic starting to blister.

It was kind of like a science project. Until now, I'd never thought about what was inside one of those cords. Of course, it made sense. Wire was stronger than plastic and something that got pulled so often had to be strong.

Jewel's voice brought me back to what was happening on the bus. "That is so disgusting," she said. First I thought she meant the smell of the burnt plastic, but then I realized she was pointing at Kelly and Jake. I peered between the seats in front of me for a better look. All I could see were the tops of their heads, but I was pretty sure the two of them were making out.

Lucky Jake, I thought.

And poor Georgie.

Georgie was coughing now too.

Someone—I didn't see who—threw an apple toward the back of the bus.

When Georgie caught it, his face relaxed for a second. He looked at the apple as if he was deciding whether he wanted to bite into it.

Maybe Georgie wasn't hungry. Maybe the apple had too many brown spots, or maybe Georgie felt bad about Kelly and Jake, and he just felt like throwing something. I wasn't surprised when he leaned over to open a window and got ready to hurl the apple out the window.

"Hey, Georgie!" someone called out. "Watch out for that little old lady on the curb!"

Jewel Chu cleared her throat. "Excuse me, Kelly," she shouted, "but are you and Jake going out now?"

That's when Georgie threw the apple out the window—hard. I could tell from his eyes he was aiming for the old lady. I bit my lip as I watched the apple sail through the air. I didn't want the old lady

53

to get hurt, but I have to admit I felt excited at the same time. A guy never knew what could happen next on the 121 Express.

The apple grazed the side of the old lady's head. Her lips made an *O* before she went clattering down to the ground.

Jewel's face was pressed up against the glass. "Oh my god!" she shrieked. "That poor old lady! I think she fainted—or worse!"

Georgie wiped his forehead with the back of his hand. I guess he hadn't expected his aim to be so good. "It was just a little apple," he said, watching as a small crowd formed a circle around the lady.

"The size of the apple doesn't matter," Sandeep said in a loud voice. "What matters is the velocity the apple achieved when it was flying in the air. Velocity is a function of—"

Sandeep must have realized he sounded like a loser, because he stopped himself in mid-sentence.

At least Jake and Kelly had quit making out. Kelly turned and gave Georgie a look that said he deserved to suffer.

A couple of people were helping the old lady up from the sidewalk. One woman took hold of her elbow; someone else picked up her purse. The apple rolled off the curb and landed at the side of the road.

"See, she's fine!" Georgie said. "I told you. It was just a little apple."

The old lady pointed at the apple, and a man standing nearby picked it up and handed it to her. I watched as she slipped it into her purse. Evidence, I thought, but I didn't say it out loud. I didn't want to upset Georgie.

But Georgie was busy clicking his lighter. I started clicking mine too.

I remembered how I'd felt when that guy whose car I'd splattered with yogurt got on the bus. I figured Georgie could use a little support.

"We should check to see that the woman is all right," Sandeep said. His voice cracked a bit.

"What are you? A paramedic or something?" Pierre shouted.

"I told you she's fine. It was just a little apple," said Georgie.

The way Georgie kept saying that made me think he was more upset than he was letting on.

A couple of the people who'd been milling around the old lady looked up at the bus. An old man stamped his cane on the sidewalk.

Pierre stuck his head out the window. "You senile or what?"

The bus driver muttered to himself. Though I couldn't hear what he was saying, I was pretty sure he was cursing us out. But today he didn't seem to have the energy to yell or make us walk home. He just kept driving and muttering away like a madman.

Sometimes I wondered what the guy had done to get assigned to the 121 Express. It wasn't like he was young and just starting out. Maybe his supervisor wanted to punish him. If that was the case, the plan seemed to be working.

When we reached the metro station, Georgie made sure to let Jake and Kelly get off the bus before him.

"You okay, man?" I asked him.

"Course I am. It was just a little apple."

Later, when it was almost my stop, I bumped into Valerie. "Oh, it's you," she said, drawing away from me as if I was contagious. "Your friends are total jerks."

Sandeep looked up from his book. "Yeah," he said. "Total jerks."

I looked at both of them. "At least I've got friends."

Valerie glared. Sandeep sucked in his breath.

But I didn't care. I didn't want anything to do with those two losers.

Chapter Eight

We were pretty surprised when Old Quack Quack—that's what everyone at Lorne Crest calls the principal, Mr. Mallard—got on the bus.

Kelly, who was drawing a heart on the side of Jake's neck, dropped her pen. Pierre, who was fiddling with the emergency window on the ceiling, dropped back into his seat.

Old Quack Quack was going bald, but he had a tuft of gray hair that grew up like a bushy island on the top of his forehead. His pop eyes bulged behind his thick glasses.

He cleared his throat. Old Quack Quack generally didn't have much to do with us students. He spent most of his time on the phone in his office.

Old Quack Quack's eyes traveled down the bus, starting at the front and working their way steadily to the back. "In August, each of you received a copy of a letter sent to me by the Montreal Transit Corporation. In that letter, the MTC threatened to stop service on the 121 Express because of complaints about bad behavior on the bus. But this time, you people have gone even further," he said, wagging a pudgy finger in the air. "Even further."

None of us said a thing. We all just sat there, trying to look innocent.

"I think you know exactly what I'm getting at," he added.

There was still no reaction. Old Quack Quack's eyes got even bulgier.

"Yesterday," he said, pausing as if he wanted to emphasize the word, "one of you threw an apple at a woman on Côte-Vertu Boulevard." Now he reached into his pocket and took out an apple—a small red MacIntosh with green speckles.

Georgie slouched in his seat as if he wished he could disappear.

"Well," Old Quack Quack went on, "it turns out that woman was seriously hurt. She sustained an injury to her eye, and the damage may be"—he lowered his voice— "permanent."

"Oh no!" Jewel Chu said, covering her mouth.

Old Quack Quack smiled approvingly at Jewel. "Oh yes," he said. "And now, I've got someone I'd like you

61

people to meet. Someone you may recognize."

There was one loud gasp on the bus—the sound of all of us gasping at the same time—when the old woman stepped onto the bus. We'd been so focused on Old Quack Quack's speech we hadn't noticed her standing outside with Mr. Adams.

She was wearing the same cloth coat she'd worn the day before, only now she had a black patch on one eye.

Old Quack Quack reached for the woman's hand and helped her up the stairs.

"Boys and girls," he said. "I'd like you to meet Annabelle Miller. Mrs. Miller—welcome to the 121 Express."

Annabelle Miller peered at us with her good eye.

I noticed Valerie scoot over in her seat so she could get a closer look at Mrs. Miller.

"Shouldn't you be lying down, Mrs. Miller? Resting your eye?" Jewel Chu asked.

Mrs. Miller shook her head. "My eye isn't very good," she said. Her voice was low, and we all leaned forward to hear her. "The doctor thinks there is a chance I'll get my vision back. But that isn't why I came here today."

She had grabbed onto one of the poles for support.

"I came here to ask you young people to stop your shenanigans. And I came here to ask you—all of you—to tell this nice young fellow," she smiled up at Old Quack Quack, "who threw the apple that hit me. Justice," she said, peering at us with her good eye, "must be served."

Old Quack Quack—imagine someone calling him young—shifted from one foot to the other. "If no one comes forward, you'll all be punished," he said. "All of you."

But no one said a thing.

Not Georgie. Not even Sandeep—or Jewel Chu.

The screaming started almost as soon as Old Quack Quack and Mrs. Miller got off the bus. "We're all gonna die!" Pierre yelled.

Kelly was bouncing up and down on Jake's lap.

"Quack! Quack!" Jake shouted.

"Did you see that hairy spot on his forehead? It looks like a toilet seat cover!" Pierre called out.

Only Georgie wasn't saying anything.

Suddenly, he sprang up from his seat and walked into the aisle. "Gimmee some room," he said, stretching his arms out in front and then behind him. The kids in the aisle pressed closer to the windows.

Georgie was only a couple of inches away from me. I didn't know what he was up to when he leaned forward and dropped his head between his knees. Then he started breathing really fast, like he was hyperventilating. He kept his head down for a minute, but then he lifted it up really quickly.

"Choke me," he whispered.

"No way, man," I told him.

"Go for it! Choke him!" voices called out—I didn't know whose.

"Uh, I don't think so," I said.

"Choke me!" Georgie insisted.

So I put my hands around Georgie's throat and choked him, just like he'd told me to. Only I didn't choke him very hard.

When he fell to the floor, his face was white as a sheet.

"Oh my god," Jewel Chu shrieked. "You killed him! You killed Georgie!"

I felt this lump—it felt as big as that MacIntosh apple Georgie had thrown at the old lady—form in my throat.

I couldn't take my eyes off Georgie's face. His pupils had slid over to the corners of his eyes. I felt my heart sinking in my chest. What had I done?

Please be okay, Georgie, I thought, please. And that's when I made a promise to myself: I was through with troublemaking.

Georgie was breathing, but only lightly.

Then all of a sudden, his lips twisted a little, and then he smirked. "I had you there, didn't I, Lucas?" he said.

I was so relieved, I could have cried. But what would my friends think if I started bawling like a baby? So I took a deep breath and laughed instead.

Chapter Nine

I was so afraid I'd killed Georgie I didn't even notice when the bus squealed to a halt. This time, the driver didn't bother pulling over to the side of the road—he stopped plunk in the middle of Côte-Vertu Boulevard, across from the McDonald's. He stopped so suddenly that a couple of kids standing in the aisle toppled into each other, and a backpack went flying and hit someone in the head. Whoever got hit yelled, "Ow!" and some of the girls at the front screamed.

Cars were honking all around us. A man in a nearby car lowered his window. "What the hell is wrong with you?" he shouted at the driver.

A woman crossing Côte-Vertu Boulevard whipped a sheet of paper from her purse. "I'm taking down your license number," she yelled, "and reporting you to the transit authorities. You could have endangered the lives of those poor innocent children!"

That cracked us up. Us—poor and innocent?

The driver just sat, hunched in his seat, running his fingers through his wispy hair. After a few seconds like that, he slid open the window next to his seat. "Go ahead and report me!" he hollered at the woman, who was still standing there, scowling.

Then, just like that, he started to laugh. It was the same haunted laugh I remembered.

Some people's laughs make you want to laugh too, even if you don't know what's so funny. But not this guy's.

Kelly raised her eyebrows. Jake shrugged. Even Jewel Chu looked confused.

A few seconds later, the driver sprung up from his seat like a Jack-in-the-Box, and Jewel Chu shrieked, "You scared me!"

The driver's eyes darted from one point to another as if he couldn't decide where he wanted to look—up at the ceiling, out to the street, or down to the floor. He'd stopped laughing, but now his cheek was twitching like crazy.

"This...this is the last straw!" he shouted, sputtering as he spoke. "The very very last. In all my life—and I'm not a young man—I have never ever met such a miserable bunch of kids. The word *monsters* isn't bad enough to describe you. You're demons. Demons!"

His voice grew more shrill with every word, and his dark eyes flashed like the blade of a knife.

"Hey, don't freak out on us, man!" Jake called out.

"Just because you're having a bad day doesn't mean you should take it out on us!" Pierre added.

Kelly bounced up from Jake's lap. "Yeah, maybe you're upset because your wife doesn't love you anymore!"

Now the driver's chest and arms were shaking. He lumbered down the aisle, stopping only when he got to where Kelly and Jake were sitting. "How dare you?" he said, looking straight at Kelly. "How dare you say something like that?"

Pierre made a snorting sound. "Maybe she's right about you and your old lady!"

The driver's knuckles were white. I don't think I'd ever seen anybody so angry. Kelly and Pierre shouldn't have said anything about his wife. Maybe it was a sensitive subject.

Somebody had to do something to calm this guy down. And it looked like that somebody was going to be me. Besides, hadn't I sworn that my trouble-making days were through?

"Look," I said, getting up from my seat, "they were just kidding. They didn't mean anything by it. Isn't that true, you guys?"

"It's true," Jake said. "We were just kidding."

Kelly giggled.

But her giggles set the driver off all over again. I guess he felt like she was laughing at him. "You're monsters! You're demons!" he shouted, even louder than before. "You have no respect! No respect at all!"

Now Jewel Chu popped up from her seat. "Excuse me, sir," she said, stopping to clear her throat, "but do you mind letting me off the bus? I'm feeling a little uncomfortable."

A couple of other kids at the front stood up too.

But the driver ignored Jewel and her friends. Now he was yelling so hard that saliva was pooling in the corners of his mouth. "I suppose you learn a lot of things in that school of yours, but one thing you haven't learned is respect. You demons have no respect for anybody!"

Just as he said the word *anybody*, his voice cracked. It was probably from all the shouting. His mouth was still moving, but no sounds came out.

Georgie was the first to laugh. But then other kids started laughing too. Not because anything was so funny, but more because they didn't know what else to do. It wasn't exactly your ordinary, everyday situation.

Our bus driver was having a meltdown—and it was our fault.

The laughter seemed to bother the driver even more than our bad behavior. The next thing he did took us all by surprise.

He crumpled on the floor, his hands wrapped around his shoulders, hugging himself. Then he sat on the floor like that and wept. His barrel chest heaved up and down, but still, he made no sound.

It was the most pathetic thing I'd ever seen.

Jewel must have figured out how to use the door mechanism, because suddenly the front and back doors popped opened.

"Let's get the hell outta this insane asylum!" Jake shouted.

Kids started stampeding out both sets of doors.

"So you'll call me, right, Jakey?" Kelly shouted from the street.

"Don't forget the French *dictée* tomorrow!" someone else called out.

More cars honked.

Kids stepped around the driver, who'd started rocking himself.

Only Sandeep stopped to talk to him. "Excuse me, sir," he said. He sounded embarrassed. "But is there anything I can do to help?"

The driver shook his head no. His cheeks were wet from crying.

Sandeep put his arm under the driver's shoulder and helped him back into his seat. "I'm going to call for help," he told him. "And I'll wait with you till someone comes."

Georgie smacked Sandeep's arm as we got off the bus. "Suck-up!" Georgie muttered.

"At least now raghead's got a friend," Pierre added.

Sandeep winced. I was starting to regret I'd ever called him raghead. I hadn't expected the name to stick.

The driver was hunched over in his seat, his head in his hands. Sandeep patted his back like he was a baby.

The whole thing was sad and funny at the same time. Maybe more sad than funny. I turned back to look at the driver before I stepped off the bus. "Take care, man," I whispered.

But I couldn't tell whether or not he'd heard me.

Chapter Ten

Lance Armstrong was my idea. "Even after he had cancer, the guy won the Tour de France—seven times," I'd told Sandeep.

Mr. Adams had paired Sandeep and me up for the modern-day heroes project. We had to choose a hero and then present him—or her—to the class.

Sandeep and I were having trouble agreeing on a hero. We'd been discussing it since last period. We'd walked out of school together and now, since we were lined up next to each other at the bus stop, we'd picked up the conversation again. "Some people say Lance Armstrong took steroids," Sandeep said. "Heroes don't take drugs."

Sandeep had a point.

But I wasn't ready to give up quite so easily. "Just because people say something, doesn't make it true. Besides, heroes don't have to be perfect."

"They don't have to be perfect; they have to be decent—and fair," Sandeep said. "If he did use steroids, it wouldn't have been fair to the other cyclists. What about Tenzing Norgay? He was the Nepalese mountaineer who reached the summit of Mount Everest with Edmund Hillary on May 29, 1953."

77

"How do you know stuff like that?"

"I like trivia. And I have a good memory."

"If we do Tenzing Norgay, then why not Edmund Hillary too? Mr. Adams said one hero only per group. So that pretty much rules out old Tenzing."

The bus pulled up to the curb. Jake had fallen asleep during English, so Mr. Adams kept him in after class, but now I spotted him rushing out of the building. He waved in my direction.

"Look," I told Sandeep, taking a few steps away from him, "let's both do some more research tonight. Then we can talk about it again tomorrow—in class."

Sandeep's eyes met mine. "I see," he said.

Jake clapped me on the shoulder. "So you and raghead hanging out now?"

I took another step away from Sandeep. "Nah," I said, "we got stuck

together on that English project is all.
We're still deciding on a hero."

Georgie's music was blaring when we
got on the bus. Pierre had already pried
open the ceiling window. Kelly, who'd
been chewing gum, blew a big pink
bubble that somehow ended up bursting
in Jewel's hair. "You get it out of my hair
this instant!" Jewel shouted.

"I can't. It's stuck!" Then Kelly
started laughing hysterically.

"You could try rubbing ice on it,"
Sandeep suggested.

Jewel put her face right up to Kelly's.
"You're evil!"

"Fight! Fight!" voices chanted from
the back of the bus. Other kids started
clapping.

There was so much noise, we almost
didn't see Old Quack Quack at the curb.
It was hard to tell who noticed him, but
suddenly Jewel popped back into her seat,

and the yelling and clapping came to a halt.

Old Quack Quack was rubbing his temples. He must've heard us from outside the bus. "I'll just be a minute or two," he told the driver.

"Good afternoon, ladies and gentlemen. I'm going to need to see three of you—in private."

The tension on the bus was so strong you could feel it in the air, like a giant bubble about to burst.

What was Old Quack Quack talking about?

Who were the three kids he wanted to see? And was I one of them?

Old Quack Quack took a sheet of lined paper from his jacket pocket. "Jake Adams," he said, his voice dull, as if he was just waking up after a long nap.

I looked over at Jake, who was pushing Kelly off his lap.

"Georgie Papadopoulos."

Georgie groaned.

My heart thumped.

"And Lucas Samson. I'm afraid the three of you won't be riding the 121 Express today."

When we got up from our seats, the bus was completely still. Most of the kids kept their eyes on the floor. But Jewel Chu smiled when we passed her.

Sandeep was the only one who actually said something. But what he said had nothing to do with our getting in trouble. "How about Rosa Parks?" he whispered to me.

Rosa Parks? What was Sandeep talking about? And then it dawned on me: Rosa Parks was a modern-day hero. She had something to do with the American civil rights movement.

Leave it to Sandeep to be thinking about our English project. I sure wasn't thinking about school. And I wasn't even thinking about how upset my parents were going to be when they found out I'd gotten in trouble. No, I was only thinking about one thing. It was the same thing everyone on the bus—except Sandeep—was thinking about.

Who was the snitch?

Chapter Eleven

Old Quack Quack called our punish-
ment "community service," but we
knew it was just his way of getting free
labor: He was making the three of us
paint the lockers.

At least we still got to ride the 121
Express.

The new bus driver had a face like
stone. He didn't show any reaction when

we got on the bus on Monday afternoon. And he didn't say a word when Georgie didn't show him his bus pass. He kept his eyes on the road and paid no attention to our screaming and fighting.

"The other driver was way more fun," Kelly said. "At least he noticed us."

Even though Kelly was still going out with Jake, she was back on speaking terms with Georgie, who sat with Pierre in the seat behind the two lovebirds.

"Kelly," Georgie said, "I've got this really cool idea." Then he dropped his voice. "How'd you like to play a little trick on raghead?"

I groaned—but only to myself. Couldn't these guys find something better to do than torment Sandeep?

"This trick you're talking about," Kelly said to Georgie, "what's in it for me?"

"How does ten bucks sound?"

"What do I have to do?"

"Just kiss him—on the lips."

"Eww," Kelly said, "there's no way. Besides, Jake wouldn't like it, would you, Jakey?" If Jake didn't like being called Jakey, he didn't let on.

Georgie leaned forward. "It'd just be a joke," he said, slapping his thigh. "Imagine how old raghead'll react! Getting kissed by a hot girl like you! The guy'll think he got sent to heaven. Besides, Jake wouldn't mind, would you Jake? I mean it's not like you own Kelly."

Kelly crossed her arms over her chest. "Of course he doesn't own me."

"Do it if you want," Jake said. "I guess it could be kind of funny."

"Ten bucks?" Kelly asked. "How 'bout fifteen?"

Georgie turned to face the rest of us. "What do you guys say? Anyone want to put up another five?"

"I'll do it," Pierre said, pulling a five-dollar bill out and handing it to Georgie.

Phew, I thought. It was a mean prank, and I was relieved I wasn't going to be part of it. Besides, I'd sworn off troublemaking. What kind of guy was I if I couldn't keep a promise I'd made to myself?

"Do you want me to do it now?" Kelly asked.

Georgie and Pierre nodded.

Kelly didn't just walk over to the front of the bus. She sauntered over like she was a movie star. She took really small steps and her hips swiveled the whole way.

Part of me felt bad for Sandeep. But I had to admit another part of me was looking forward to seeing how embarrassed he'd be. In a way, the guy had it coming. This is what he gets for acting like he's so much smarter than the rest of us.

I moved to the edge of my seat to get a better view. As usual, Sandeep had his nose in a textbook. Georgie and Pierre were already laughing.

When Kelly said, "Hey, Sandeep," Sandeep nearly dropped his book. Even from where I was sitting, I could see him blush. It looked like he was trying to say something back to Kelly, only he couldn't.

"I've got something for you, Sandeep. It's a little present from your friends at the back of the bus." Kelly tossed her blond hair in our direction. When she leaned toward Sandeep, he moved away. What kind of guy who was about to be kissed by the hottest girl on the 121 Express would do that?

But Kelly was quicker than him. She leaned over so her chest was right where Sandeep's book had been—and kissed him smack on the lips.

Jewel Chu's eyes looked like they were about to pop out of her head.

"Are you going out with him, now?" she asked.

Kelly turned to face Jewel. "Maybe," she said. "Or maybe not."

Everyone cracked up. This was the funniest thing that had happened on the bus in weeks. Maybe that's why we didn't notice when Sandeep started making weird gulping noises.

But Jewel noticed. "I think he's having an allergic reaction," she shouted.

Sandeep's dark skin had become much paler and he had a panicked look in his eyes. It looked like he was trying to swallow, but there was something caught in his throat.

"He's pointing at something!" Kelly called out. She was still standing in the aisle, only now she looked embarrassed. I guess she didn't like the idea of a guy being allergic to her—even if the guy was Sandeep.

Sandeep's hand was trembling, but Jewel was right, he was pointing across the aisle to where Valerie was sitting.

"It's your brown bag!" Jewel yelled. "I think he wants your brown bag."

Valerie dumped the contents of her bag on the floor—a bruised banana and a bag of chips—and threw the bag over to Kelly, who gave it to Sandeep.

Sandeep leaned over the bag, and I was sure he was going to vomit into it—the way people do when they get motion sickness on an airplane. But he just breathed into the bag, taking long deep breaths until he returned to normal.

"Are you okay?" Kelly asked.

Sandeep just kept breathing into the bag.

"Maybe he really is allergic to you," Jewel said.

Sandeep's reaction pretty much took the fun out of the whole plan. Kelly refused to take Georgie's fifteen bucks.

"Keep your money," she said. "It was a dumb idea anyway."

Even after Sandeep folded up the brown bag, he wouldn't look up.

"What'd you do? Drop your physics notes on the floor?" Jake called out.

Kelly smacked Jake's arm. "Don't give him a hard time," she said.

We hit every red light on the way from the Côte-Vertu metro station to our stop. When Sandeep stood up, I got up and followed him to the front of the bus. "You okay?" I asked.

Sandeep raised his eyes from the floor. "Ever notice how you only talk to me when your pals aren't around?" he said. "Why do you think that is?"

I shrugged. "I was just asking is all."

"I'm okay," Sandeep said.

When the bus stopped, he rushed out and headed down the street.

Now it was just me and the driver. I turned to face him. He looked much younger than the last driver—but maybe that was only because he was new to the route. Maybe we'd age this guy too. "What happened to our last driver?" I asked.

"Breakdown," he said, without looking up from the wheel and making it sound as if it was the most natural thing in the world. "Nervous collapse. It's a shame too. That guy was a real fighter in the bus drivers' union. We could always count on him to stand up for the rest of us."

Chapter Twelve

Jewel Chu snickered when I passed her on my way to the back of the bus. "You've got paint stains on the bottom of your pants!"

As if I hadn't noticed.

Jake, Georgie and I had spent lunch and recess painting lockers. My back ached from the work and my whole body stank of turpentine. But there was some good news: Annabelle Miller had got her vision back, and we'd be finished painting the lockers by the end of the week.

Of course, we had to put up with a bit of teasing.

"I heard Old Quack Quack tell the viceprincipal that when you guys are done, he's gonna have you come to his house and paint the garage," Kelly said.

Jake pushed the hair out of his eyes. "Tell me you're kidding."

Kelly burst into laughter. We figured that meant she was kidding.

Teasing someone was way more fun than getting teased.

At least Sandeep and I had finally agreed on a hero—or as it turned out, a heroine. We'd decided to do our presentation on Rosa Parks, after all. I was right about her having something to do with the American civil rights movement. Mrs. Parks had fought against racial discrimination on the city buses in Montgomery, Alabama. In 1955, Mrs. Parks refused to give up her seat on the bus to a white person. And as far as we knew, she'd never been accused of taking steroids.

Valerie tapped my elbow as I made my way down the aisle. "I think it's cool you guys chose a woman as your hero. It shows you're progressive."

I was so surprised she'd talked to me that I didn't know what to say. "Uh, thanks," I managed to mutter.

Jake narrowed his eyes when he saw me talking to Valerie. "I bet you anything she's the snitch," he said when I got to the back of the bus. "Haven't you seen her writing in that little note-book she's got? She probably records our every move so she and Old Quack Quack have something to talk about."

Georgie was just as sure it was Sandeep. "Remember how we got Kelly to humiliate him? Sandeep is the only one with a motive. The guy hates our guts."

"You're not making any sense, Georgie," Kelly said, shaking her head. "That thing with Sandeep happened after Old Quack Quack pulled the three of you off the bus."

I suggested Jewel Chu. "She's the biggest goody-goody on the bus."

"You mean the smallest," Jake said.

I couldn't say the three of us had been on the best behavior since our run-in with Old Quack Quack. But definitely better behavior. For one thing, we'd stopped throwing things at people—or their cars. Old Quack Quack had heard about the field berry yogurt and he wasn't too impressed.

The new driver was still ignoring us. He seemed to be able to tune out our shouting, and the smell of burnt plastic didn't seem to bug him.

"I know this sounds crazy, but I kind of miss the old driver," Jake said as the bus turned onto Côte-Vertu Boulevard.

I understood how Jake felt.

Pierre was busy emptying his backpack. "What in the world are you doing?" Kelly asked.

"Getting rid of my math notes."

We'd had a math test that afternoon. Geometry.

Kelly raised her eyebrows. "Can't you do that at home?"

"It wouldn't be as much fun. Besides, Mr. Adams said we were done studying triangles."

Pierre was shredding his notes. When he opened the window, we knew straightaway what he was up to. Jake and I looked at each other—and grinned. Pierre had a knack for coming up with zany schemes.

Georgie nodded from across the aisle. "It's just paper. It can't hurt anybody."

Soon everyone at the back of the bus was ripping up their math notes and throwing them out the windows. "It's like confetti!" Kelly shouted as she watched her notes take off in a gust of wind.

"You guys are littering!" Jewel Chu shouted.

I'd had it with her. Who did she think she was—the police? "What are you going to do—tell on us again?" I shouted back.

Jewel jumped up from her seat so quickly her glasses nearly fell off her nose. "I'm not the snitch!"

"If you're not, who is?" Jake yelled.

The bus went quiet. Even the bus driver was watching the action in his rearview mirror.

Jewel adjusted her glasses. "All I know is, it's not me."

I figured it was a good time to watch the other suspects' faces. Unfortunately, Sandeep's was hidden behind a textbook. Had he done that on purpose? Valerie's notebook was out. Maybe Jake was right and she was the snitch after all. I hoped not.

"Come on!" Pierre shouted. "Who's still got notes to get rid of?"

"I do!" I'd been so busy getting upset with Jewel I hadn't taken my math notes out of my backpack. Just as I lifted my backpack from the floor, I remembered the promise I'd made to myself. But Georgie was right: A little paper couldn't hurt anybody.

Besides, tearing up the notes felt good. I wanted to wait for a good gust of wind so my notes would fly up into the air the way Kelly's had. I didn't have to wait long.

I watched as the notes rose in the air. For a second or two, they made a sort of triangle—with an acute angle. Mr. Adams would like that. He was always saying how important it is to apply what you learn at school to the real world.

When the wind died down, my notes dropped to the pavement. I leaned out the window and watched as one car drove over them, then another. Good riddance, I thought.

Chapter Thirteen

Georgie unzipped his backpack. Then he turned around to make sure we were the only ones who could see inside. "Look what I've got," he whispered.

I saw the flash of metal before I realized what it was.

Jake shrugged. "Big deal! It's just a pair of scissors. What'd you do—raid your mother's sewing basket?"

Pierre nudged Georgie. "You making yourself a new dress?" he asked.

"I don't look good in dresses. But I thought of something else we could do with these scissors. Something fun." Georgie raised his eyebrows toward the front of the bus, where Sandeep was sitting.

Why did these guys want to keep picking on Sandeep? Did they really think he was the snitch?

"So what's your plan?" Pierre asked.

"My plan is we give the guy a haircut. Sikhs don't believe in haircuts. It's against their religion or something."

Jake snickered. "I'm beginning to see your point. Raghead needs a trim."

"Exactly."

The four of us were huddled together, like football players reviewing their game plan. Usually, I liked hanging out like this with my buddies, but now I had a sick feeling in my stomach.

"So what do we do?" Pierre asked.

"We're gonna have to get his turban off first." Georgie looked up at me. "That's where you come in, Lucas."

"I do?"

"Uh-huh. You're gonna distract him. Go talk to him about Rosa Parks or something."

Hearing Rosa Parks's name made me feel even worse. We'd picked Rosa Parks because she'd stood up against racial discrimination, and here I was going along with a plan to discriminate against Sandeep for being Sikh.

I tried to think of some way to talk them out of it. "What if he starts hyperventilating again?" I asked.

Georgie rolled his eyes. "We'll get him a paper bag. It did the trick last time." Then Georgie pressed his palm down on my right shoulder. It didn't hurt, but it didn't feel right, either. "Go for it, man," he said.

Then he gave me a push that sent me flying down the crowded aisle.

Kelly winked when I passed her. Was she was just being friendly or did she know about Georgie's plan?

The driver stopped for a red light.

Jewel and one of her friends waved at a guy in the next car. "He's really cute," Jewel's friend said.

"And he looks nice."

"Who cares about nice?"

When the guy waved back, the two girls fell to the floor, laughing. I had to step over the heap they made on the floor.

I looked up ahead. Sandeep's nose wasn't buried in a book. He was staring out the window. But he must have felt me coming because he looked up. He lifted one hand as if he was about to wave at me, but then he seemed to change his mind.

I knew Sandeep wasn't the snitch. And I knew he wasn't a bad guy. And I knew it would be wrong to cut his hair. He was entitled to his beliefs—just like people, no matter what color skin they had, were entitled to any seat on a bus.

I heard loud laughter coming from behind me. I didn't have to turn around to know it was Georgie—with his backpack and his mother's sewing scissors.

"Hey, Lucas, get a move on!" Jake called from behind him.

"Yeah, Lucas, let's go!" Pierre shouted.

I was only about a foot away from Sandeep. His eyebrows were raised, as if he couldn't quite figure out why I'd come all the way to the front of the bus to talk to him—when all my friends were watching.

Sandeep moved in a little closer to the guy sitting next to him. It took me a second to realize he was making room for me to sit down.

I put out my hand to stop him. "That's okay," I said. "I'm not gonna sit."

I could hear Georgie chuckling behind me.

Sandeep shook his head. I could tell he was confused. His eyes kept darting between me and Georgie. Sandeep must have sensed something was up. Something mean. He straightened his back.

That's when I knew I couldn't let my friends go ahead with their plan. This was one of those defining moments my mom had been talking about. I had to stand up—not just for Sandeep, but for myself too.

I thought about Rosa Parks and what must have been going on inside her head when she refused to give up her seat to a white person. She must have been scared. But I bet she was angry too.

And she must have known she was doing the right thing—and that gave her courage.

I needed some of Rosa Parks's courage.

I wasn't standing up against something big, like segregation, the way Rosa Parks had. But I was standing up for something I believed in. I wasn't going to get thrown into prison like Rosa Parks, but I was risking something too. By tomorrow, I might be sitting up here with the losers. Permanently.

"Hey, Sandeep."

"Hey, Lucas."

Georgie was pressing in behind me snapping the scissors.

That's when I sprung around. Georgie's eyes widened. "What ya doing, man?"

"Give me the scissors," I said. "Now." My voice sounded braver than I felt.

Georgie's dark eyes grew even darker. "No way."

I tried to grab the scissors from him. But Georgie wouldn't let go.

"Fight! Fight!" voices called.

Kids rushed over from the back of the bus.

"One of them is armed!" Jewel Chu shouted.

I turned to Sandeep. "Open the window. Quick!"

The scissors scratched the back of my hand, but I managed to wrestle them away from Georgie. I knew I had to get rid of them, before something bad happened. "Is there anyone out there? Any cars— any people?" My voice was cracking.

Sandeep turned to look out the window. "No," he said, "no cars, no people."

So I tossed the scissors out the window. They made a clanging noise when they hit the pavement.

Georgie was so angry he was shaking. "Why'd you do that, you jerk?" he shouted. "We were supposed to be having fun."

Jake grabbed my shoulders. "Yeah, what's wrong with you Lucas?"

I shook myself loose from his grip. "You guys don't get it, do you? How come your idea of fun always means someone has to get hurt or humiliated? It's wrong. Plain wrong. And I've had enough."

Someone clapped. It was probably Jewel. My cheeks felt hot.

Georgie put his hands on his hips, looked straight at me and laughed. Jake and Pierre laughed too. Pierre raised a finger to his forehead and made the shape of an L. "You're a loser, man," he said.

Pierre was so close I could hear him breathing.

"I'll take that as a compliment."

Chapter Fourteen

WHO'S THE SNITCH?

Kelly had used her finger to write the words on the back window. It had been pouring all day. The inside of the bus felt muggy, and the windows were misted over.

I headed to the middle. The guys at the back were ignoring me—and I'd turned down Sandeep's offer to sit with him. He didn't understand that just because I'd stood up for him didn't mean I wanted to be his best friend.

But when Valerie patted the empty spot next to her, I'd taken it. As I peeled off my windbreaker, I caught a whiff of her shampoo. It smelled like apples. There might be some advantages, I thought, to standing up for what you believed in.

It was the same seat I'd taken when I first rode the 121 Express. Of course, a lot had changed since then. For one thing, I'd made friends—and for another, I'd lost them.

Kelly was still busy writing on the window. She was working on a list of suspects. Jewel's name was first; Sandeep's was second.

Jewel threw her hands up in the air. "Why do I get blamed for every-thing?" The funny thing was she didn't sound upset. Maybe Jewel was the snitch—or maybe she just liked the attention.

Sandeep didn't lift his eyes from his physics textbook.

"Put Lucas's name up there too!" Pierre called out.

I felt my heart bump in my chest. I didn't like how Pierre and the others were ignoring me, but accusing me of being the snitch was worse. Way worse.

Kelly didn't turn around. Her fingertip was pressed against the glass—poised to write. "Lucas can't be the snitch," she said. "He's one of the guys who got turned in. Remember?"

"You never know…" When Pierre raised his voice I knew he wanted me to hear him. "Maybe he had it all planned out. Maybe Lucas isn't as dumb as he looks. What was it Mr. Adams called him?"

"Brainiac!" Jake shouted.

"Yeah, Brainiac might have master-minded the whole thing."

I thought about taking out a textbook and hiding behind it—like Sandeep. My cover was blown. Now everyone would know about the Brainiac thing.

In the end, it was Valerie who rescued me. "Take a look at this picture I found of Mahatma Gandhi," she said. When she leaned in to show me the picture, the top of her head touched the side of my arm. There was something about the color of her hair that made me forget— for a few seconds, anyhow—how lousy I was feeling.

But then Pierre's soccer ball came flying through the air and hit the side of my head. Instead of complaining, I used my palm to send the ball back to Pierre.

"Are those Mentos?" I heard Georgie call out.

"You hate Mentos, Georgie," Kelly said.

"I need them for a…a science experiment is all."

Jake laughed. "A science experiment? Who do you think you are? Raghead? Or the Brainiac?"

Everyone turned to see what Georgie was up to—even Sandeep put down his book. I turned to look too.

Georgie had a small bottle of Diet Coke in his hands. He opened it up and handed Jake the plastic bottle cap. "Hey, do me a favor and make a hole in the cap. Now, okay?"

"Hey, do I look like your lab assistant?" Jake said, but he used his pen to puncture the cap and gave it back to Georgie.

Georgie slid something inside the bottle—it must have been one of those Mentos—and screwed the cap back on.

He put his thumb over the hole in the cap, and then he shook the bottle up and down—hard. He made a hooting sound when he released his thumb.

Pow! The bottle flew out of Georgie's hands like a rocket and zoomed across the aisle. It hit a window, ricocheted off of it, and then crashed to the floor. There was Diet Coke everywhere— on the windows, on kids' clothes and backpacks and even dribbling down Georgie's face.

"Gross! It's so sticky!" voices screamed.

Everyone was laughing, especially Georgie.

I tried not to laugh, but it was hard.

"Hey, Georgie, you should be a science teacher!" Kelly called out.

Georgie was laughing so hard that he started to cough. He covered his mouth and tried taking a few breaths, but the coughing wouldn't stop.

"Hey, raghead!" Jake called out. "Have you got a paper bag we can borrow?"

That made everyone laugh all over again.

When I turned to look at Sandeep, I expected him to be hiding behind his book, but he wasn't. He was watching Georgie.

Georgie's cheeks were apple red. When he started to wheeze, Sandeep sprang up from his seat and pushed his way over to the back of the bus.

"Open the windows!" he shouted.

Maybe because no one was used to seeing Sandeep like this—rushing around and telling other people what to do—they opened the windows.

"His lips are turning blue!" Kelly sounded as if she was about to cry.

Sandeep was hunched over Georgie. "I think his bronchial tubes are blocked with mucus. Here," he said, reaching behind Georgie's back, "try to sit up straight."

Then Sandeep lifted his head. "Has anyone here got a puffer?" he shouted.

"Don't you know you're not supposed to share medications?" Jewel said.

You'd think that with fifty kids on the 121 Express, someone would have asthma medication. But no one did. I bit my lip.

"Georgie doesn't have asthma," Kelly told Sandeep.

"I'm pretty sure he does. And it's getting worse."

Georgie was having trouble sitting up, and when he tried to say something, he nearly gagged.

"What do we do?" Kelly shouted.

"Lucas," Sandeep said, "talk to the bus driver. Tell him he's got to take us to the hospital—now!"

I bolted over to the driver. "You have to take us to the hospital. This guy at the back's having an asthma attack," I told him.

"This is another one of your games, right?" the driver muttered.

"This isn't a game. It's an emergency. And you've got to help us. Please."

When the driver took his first left instead of driving straight along Côte-Vertu Boulevard, I made a loud sigh. I hadn't realized I'd been holding my breath.

Chapter Fifteen

Georgie was back at school. The only problem was Mrs. Papadopoulos. She kept phoning to make sure he hadn't lost his puffer.

Things on the bus had changed since Georgie's asthma attack. Sure, there was still singing and screaming and fighting. Pierre sneezed into his hand and wiped it right on the pole next to him. "That is so disgusting!" Jewel Chu called out.

For once, Jake agreed with Jewel. "Haven't you ever heard of this invention called Kleenex?" he asked Pierre.

The main change on the bus was we weren't so divided up anymore. Like right now, Georgie was standing at the front, telling Sandeep he thought our presentation on Rosa Parks was pretty cool.

I was sitting near the middle of the bus. I could have sat with the guys at the back—we were on speaking terms again—but Valerie had saved a spot for me. I liked sitting next to her, and besides, these days the middle of the bus felt like the right place for me. I had friends up front—and in the back.

Even the new bus driver was getting a little friendlier. We had been through a lot together. He'd risked getting in trouble with his supervisor to get Georgie to the hospital, and once we got there, he'd helped carry Georgie into the emergency room. We had all been pretty scared when Georgie's fingernails started turning blue.

The driver had told us his name was Thomas. It's funny how things feel different once you know someone's name. I'd asked him the name of the old driver too, the one we'd driven over the edge. Thomas told me it was Gilbert Dubuc. He also told me how Gilbert Dubuc had spent a couple of weeks in a convalescent home, but that he was back at work, driving another bus. "Not the 121 Express, of course. The supervisor doesn't want him cracking up again. Anyway, it's good news for us drivers," Thomas had said. "Dubuc says by spring, he should be strong enough to get back to his work with the union. He's quite a guy, that Dubuc."

Old Quack Quack was back on the bus too. Only this time, he hadn't come to scold us. No, today he was smiling like the Cheshire Cat in *Alice's Adventures in Wonderland*.

He nodded at Georgie. "I hope you have your puffer," he said. Mrs. Papadopoulos must have spoken to him too.

I didn't think much of it when Old Quack Quack nodded at Pierre next. It was only when Valerie raised her eyebrows that I started wondering. Pierre wasn't exactly a star pupil.

"Are you thinking what I'm thinking?" Valerie whispered.

"I guess it's possible," I told Valerie. "Maybe Pierre struck some kind of deal with Old Quack Quack. Like maybe Old Quack Quack didn't phone home after Pierre blew Mr. Adams's last math quiz."

"We should tell the others," Valerie said. "Remember how everyone was accusing everyone else? A lot of feelings got hurt."

I decided not to tell her I'd thought she might have been the snitch.

Pierre had been the one to accuse me of being the snitch. Now I understood why.

"So let's tell," Valerie said.

"Nah," I said. "All that's behind us now."

Old Quack Quack cleared his throat so loudly and for so long it sounded like he was gargling. "I want to say that I'm—er—" He stopped to flatten the knot on his tie. You could tell he was more used to scolding kids than saying anything nice. "I'm—er—proud of you people. I never thought I'd say it, but there you go. You people stayed calm in a difficult situation. And that calmness, that composure, probably saved this young man's life. I also want to express my gratitude to your driver." He turned to shake Thomas's hand. "You did the right thing," Old Quack Quack told him, "by getting Georgie straight to the hospital."

And then, Old Quack Quack did something we never would have expected. He clapped—for us. And everyone on the bus started clapping too.

The clapping was followed by cheering. Then Old Quack Quack rushed off the bus.

"Calm and composed! That's us, all right!" Jake shouted as Thomas turned onto Côte-Vertu Boulevard.

Everyone was talking and laughing all at the same time.

When we stopped at the first inter-section, I almost didn't notice the bus that had pulled up across from ours. But something—don't ask me what—made me turn to look at it. I recognized the driver's thin gray hair and the way he gripped the steering wheel. It was our old driver, Gilbert Dubuc.

At first, I was too startled to say anything. But Valerie noticed him too. "Hey, you guys!" she shouted. "Look who's driving that bus!"

In the old days, someone would have pushed open a window and yelled something rude—or maybe thrown something at him.

But this wasn't the old days. I was the first to wave. Next thing I knew the other kids were waving too.

I thought I saw Gilbert Dubuc shudder. Was he remembering all the trouble we'd caused him?

But then he did something that took me by surprise. Something that made me wonder if he'd heard about how the kids on the 121 Express had helped save Georgie.

He waved back.

The Hot Dog Haven
4200 Côte-Vertu Blvd.
Ville St. Laurent, Quebec

November 6, 2007

Lorne Crest Academy
4243 Decelles Ave.
Ville St. Laurent, Quebec
Att.: John Mallard, Principal

Dear Mr. Mallard,

I am writing this letter to you out of desperation. My husband and I recently opened The Hot Dog Haven, a small restaurant behind Lorne Crest Academy. At first, we thought being located so close to a school would help our business. But now, we're not so sure. Yes, your students have been buying lunch at our restaurant. But that, dear Mr. Mallard, is not all they've been doing!

They have also been teasing our waiters and waitresses, throwing food, emptying the salt and pepper shakers into their water glasses. We have even overheard them discussing strange science experiments, and frankly, we're worried they might blow the place up!

At The Hot Dog Haven, we pride ourselves on serving the best hot dogs in all Montreal. We believe eating at our restaurant is a privilege. Please make it clear to your students that if their behavior does not improve, we shall be forced to shut our doors to them.

Sincerely yours,

Marie Therrien,
Co-proprietor,
The Hot Dog Haven

Acknowledgments

The idea for this book grew out of Quebec Roots: the Place Where I Live, an educational program run by Montreal's Blue Metropolis Literary Foundation. In 2005-2006, photographer Monique Dykstra and I worked with groups of students in three Quebec schools. Together, we helped them tell their stories in photographs and words. One class chose to explore their zany adventures on an after-school bus designated specially for them. The minute their teacher Andrew Adams told me about life on the bus, I knew my next book project had landed.

Of course, I owe a huge debt to Andrew Adams and his 2005-2006 English class for their inspiration and openheartedness. Thanks also to several of Mr. Adams's other students, who came in over lunch to share more bus stories.

Special thanks to Linda Leith, artistic director of Blue Met, Blue Met educational program coordinator Maïté de Hemptinne, as well as the rest of the Blue Met team.

As always, my friend Viva Singer was there to listen when I needed to talk out my story. My editor Melanie Jeffs also deserves special thanks for her encouragement, input and tremendous sense of fun.

A final thank-you goes to my husband Michael Shenker and my daughter Alicia Melamed—I love you both too much.

Monique Polak is the popular author of many books for juveniles and teens, including *Finding Elmo* and *121 Express* in the Orca Currents series. Monique lives in Montreal, Quebec.

orca *currents*

978-1-55469-155-5 $9.95 pb

Justin is fascinated with the aged guard dog at the corner store. He names it Smokey and sneaks the dog treats. Smokey belongs to a company that supplies working dogs to local businesses. Justin is thrilled to get a job working for Smokey's company, until he learns about the mistreatment of the animals. As the suspicious activity in the company increases, Justin starts to worry about the fate of his friend—and himself.

orca *currents*

978-1-55143-686-9 $9.95 pb

"I've come up with a plan,"
Dad said.

Phew, I thought, relaxing a little. Dad was a smart guy. I should have known he'd come up with a plan. Maybe he wanted to hang a bigger sign outside the store or advertise on the radio.

But it wasn't that at all.

"I've agreed to start renting out the big birds," Dad said. For a second, I felt like someone had kicked me in the stomach. What was Dad thinking? "For parties and conventions. It's a good way to bring in extra cash—" Here, he paused for a moment. "They want Elmo first."

Titles in the Series

orca currents

Marked
Norah McClintock

Mirror Image
K.L. Denman

Nine Doors
Vicki Grant

Perfect Revenge
K.L. Denman

Pigboy
Vicki Grant

Power Chord
Ted Staunton

Queen of the Toilet Bowl
Frieda Wishinsky

Rebel's Tag
K.L. Denman

Reckless
Lesley Choyce

See No Evil
Diane Young

Sewer Rats
Sigmund Brouwer

The Shade
K.L. Denman

Skate Freak
Lesley Choyce

Slick
Sara Cassidy

The Snowball Effect
Deb Loughead

Special Edward
Eric Walters

Splat!
Eric Walters

Spoiled Rotten
Dayle Campbell Gaetz

Storm Tide
Kari Jones

Struck
Deb Loughead

Stuff We All Get
K.L. Denman

Sudden Impact
Lesley Choyce

Swiped
Michele Martin Bossley

Watch Me
Norah McClintock

Windfall
Sara Cassidy

Wired
Sigmund Brouwer

orca *currents*

For more information on all the books
in the Orca Currents series, please visit
www.orcabook.com